c4

For Fred Rogers

Ann Beneduce, Creative Editor

The author and publisher thank Wendy Worth, Curator of Birds and Small Mammals, Zoo Atlanta, Atlanta, Georgia, for her advice and comments.

Eric Carle's name and signature logotype are trademarks of Eric Carle.

Does a Kangaroo Have a Mother, Too?
Copyright © 2000 by Eric Carle
Manufactured in China. All rights reserved.
http://www.harperchildrens.com
http://www.eric-carle.com

Library of Congress Cataloging-in Publication Data
Carle, Eric.
Does a kangaroo have a mother, too? / Eric Carle.
p.   cm.
Summary: Presents the names of animal babies, parents, and groups, for example, a baby kangaroo is a joey, its mother is a flyer, its father is a boomer, and a group of kangaroos is a troop, mob, or herd.
ISBN 0-06-028768-3. — ISBN 0-06-028767-5 (lib. bdg.)
1. Animals—Infancy—Juvenile literature. [1. Animals—Infancy.] I. Title.
QL763.C37   2000
591.3'9—dc21   99-36147   CIP

HAVE A MOTHER, TOO ?

by Eric Carle

HarperCollins*Publishers*

YES !

A **KANGAROO** has a mother.
Just like me and you.

Does a lion have a mother, too?

Yes!
A **LION** has a mother.
Just like me and you.

Does a giraffe have a mother, too?

Yes!
A **GIRAFFE** has a mother.
Just like me and you.

Does a penguin have a mother, too?

Yes!
A PENGUIN has a mother.
Just like me and you.

Does a swan have a mother, too?

Yes!
A **SWAN** has a mother.
Just like me and you.

Does a fox have a mother, too?

Yes!
A **FOX** has a mother.
Just like me and you.

Does a dolphin have a mother, too?

Yes!
A DOLPHIN has a mother.
Just like me and you.

Does a sheep have a mother, too?

Yes!
A **SHEEP** has a mother.
Just like me and you.

Does a bear have a mother, too?

Yes!
A **BEAR** has a mother.
Just like me and you.

Does an elephant have a mother, too?

Yes!
An **ELEPHANT** has a mother.
Just like me and you.

Does a monkey have a mother, too?

Yes!
A **MONKEY** has a mother.
Just like me and you.

And do animal mothers love their babies?

YES ! YES ! Of course they do.

Animal mothers love their babies,
just as yours loves you.

Names of animal babies, parents, and groups in this book

Kangaroo A baby kangaroo is a *joey*. Its mother is a *flyer* and its father is a *boomer*. A group of kangaroos is a *troop* or a *mob* or a *herd*.

Lion A baby lion is a *cub*. Its mother is a *lioness* and its father is a *lion*. A group of lions is a *pride*.

Giraffe A baby giraffe is a *calf*. Its mother is a *cow* and its father is a *bull*. A group of giraffes is a *tower* or a *herd*.

Penguin A baby penguin is a *chick*. Its mother is a *dam* and its father is a *sire*. A group of penguins is a *colony* or a *parade*.

Swan A baby swan is a *cygnet*. Its mother is a *pen* and its father is a *cob*. A group of swans is a *wedge* or a *herd*.

Fox A baby fox is a *cub* or a *pup*. Its mother is a *vixen* and its father is a *dog fox*. A group of foxes is a *pack* or a *skulk*.

Dolphin A baby dolphin is a *calf*. Its mother is a *cow* and its father is a *bull*. A group of dolphins is a *school* or a *pod*.

Sheep A baby sheep is a *lamb*. Its mother is a *ewe* and its father is a *ram*. A group of sheep is a *flock*.

Bear A baby bear is a *cub*. Its mother is a *sow* and its father is a *boar*. A group of bears is a *pack* or a *sloth*.

Elephant A baby elephant is a *calf*. Its mother is a *cow* and its father is a *bull*. A group of elephants is a *herd*.

Monkey A baby monkey is an *infant*. Its mother is a *mother* and its father is a *father*. A group of monkeys is a *group* or a *troop* or a *tribe*.

Deer A baby deer is a *fawn*. Its mother is a *doe* and its father is a *buck*. A group of deer is a *herd*.

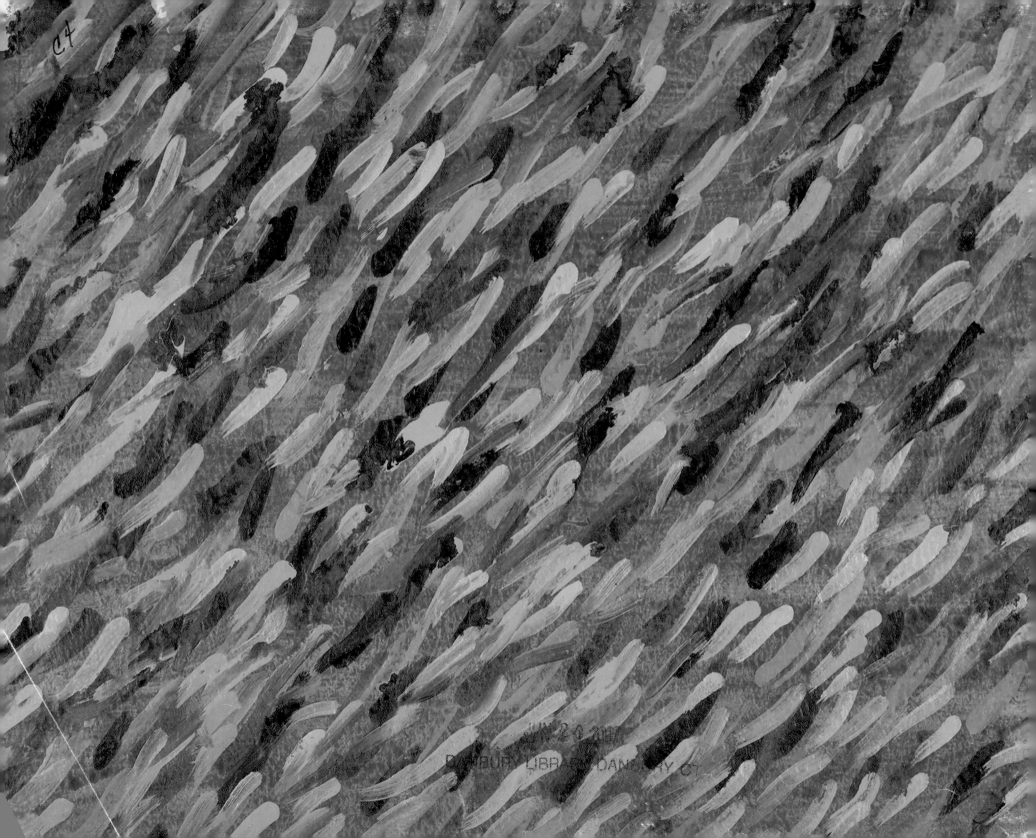